WOOF,
THE
SEEING EYE DOG

by Danae Dobson

Illustrated by Karen Loccisano

WORD PUBLISHING
Dallas·London·Vancouver·Melbourne

To my grandfather, James Dobson, Sr. He was a great man — not because he became powerful or wealthy or famous. He was great because of his deep faith in God. He prayed for me throughout my childhood and always made time to be there for me. That is why I dedicate this book to his memory.

Woof, The Seeing Eye Dog

Copyright © 1990 by Danae Dobson for the text. Copyright © 1990 by Karen Loccisano for the illustrations.

All rights reserved. No portion of this book may be reproduced in any form without the written permission of the publishers, except for brief quotations in reviews.

Library of Congress Cataloging-in-Publication Data

Dobson, Danae.
    Woof, the seeing eye dog / by Danae Dobson ; illustrated by Karen Loccisano.
      p. cm. — (The Woof series ; 8)
    Summary: After rescuing three puppies from a burning building, Woof feels too important to associate with his old friends until he fills in for a seeing-eye dog and learns that true importance comes from serving others.
    ISBN 0-8499-8363-0
    [1. Pride and vanity — Fiction. 2. Guide dogs — Fiction. 3. Dogs — Fiction. 4. Christian life — Fiction.]
  I. Loccisano, Karen, ill.
  II. Title. III. Series.
PZ7.D6614Ww   1990
  [Fic] — dc20   90-12360
                                                                CIP
                                                                AC

Printed in the United States of America
1239AGH98765432

A MESSAGE FROM
Dr. James Dobson

Before you read about this dog named Woof perhaps you would like to know how these books came to be written. When my children, Danae and Ryan, were young, I often told them stories at bedtime. Many of those tales were about pet animals who were loved by people like those in our own family. Later, I created more stories while driving the children to school in our car pool. The kids began to fall in love with these pets, even though they existed only in our minds. I found out just how much they loved these animals when I made the mistake of telling them a story in which one of their favorite pets died. There were so many tears I had to bring him back to life!

These tales made a special impression on Danae. At the age of twelve, she decided to write her own book about her favorite animal, Woof, and see if Word Publishers would like to print it. She did, and they did, and in the process she became the youngest author in Word's history. Now, ten years later, Danae has written seven more, totally new adventures with Woof and the Petersons. And she is still Word's youngest author!

Danae has discovered a talent God has given her, and it all started with our family spending time together, talking about a dog and the two children who loved him. We hope that not only will you enjoy Woof's adventures but that you and your family will enjoy the time spent reading them together. Perhaps you also will discover a talent God has given you.

It was just another ordinary day for Woof. A month
before he had rescued three puppies from a burning house
and won the hearts of the whole town of Gladstone. He had
been named "Our Favorite Hero" by the local newspaper.
And his picture was on display at the fire department. All
of this attention had caused Woof to feel pretty proud of
himself—a little *too* proud. In fact, he was becoming impos-
sible to live with.

Woof still loved the Peterson family — especially the children, Mark and Krissy. But he had begun to believe he didn't have to obey them. After all, a town hero shouldn't have to take orders from anyone!

Mark and Krissy first noticed the change when Woof refused to come when he was called. Sometimes he would even yawn and look the other way. This was not at all like the Woof they knew and loved.

Then there was the problem with his dog food. He refused to eat it! Woof felt he deserved ground hamburger, or maybe T-bone steaks, certainly more than the ordinary dog crunchies in his bowl. The town hero should eat better food than what "common" dogs are served.

It was true — Woof had changed. Just yesterday he had done something completely forbidden at the Peterson home. When the family left and forgot to put Woof outside, he jumped onto the bed and slept on the pillows. He knew it was wrong, but he thought he was worth it.

Today Woof was stretched out in the sun, pretending he didn't hear Mark call his name.

"Wow!" said ten-year-old Krissy. "Woof is really grouchy these days! He's never acted this way before."

"I know," agreed Mark, shutting the back door. "Ever since he became a hero, he hasn't been the same."

"Mother thinks he's too proud of himself," said Krissy. "He really believes he's better than everybody else."

"Remember the scripture we learned last Sunday?" asked six-year old Mark. "It says, 'Pride goes before a fall.' My Sunday school teacher said it means that when you are too proud, you sometimes get hurt. Pride makes you do bad things, and then you have to suffer for it."

Woof turned over on his back and rolled around on the grass. He could hear them talking, but he wasn't really listening. He just yawned and thought about being the town hero.

Just then Scruffy came by for a visit. He was the tiny mutt who lived in the next block. He and Woof had been friends for years, but now he wasn't welcome. Woof rudely growled and chased Scruffy from the yard. He wasn't good enough to be friends with the "town hero." As Scruffy ran down the street with tears in his eyes, Woof barked twice to tell him not to come back.

"Did you see that?" Mark asked.

"Yeah!" said Krissy. "That was a mean thing to do. I think Mom is right about Woof."

Woof *did* feel a little guilty for the way he had treated his old friend. But then, he had the right to run Scruffy away. He needed a new set of friends now that he was the "big dog" in town.

It wasn't long before Woof became bored in the back yard. Mr. Peterson had left the gate open when he left for work. So, Woof decided to go for a stroll down Maple Street. He knew he wasn't supposed to leave the yard, but he decided one short trip around the neighborhood wouldn't hurt.

Proudly, Woof trotted down the sidewalk, stopping every few seconds to sniff at a bush or a tree. He was so busy he barely noticed who was coming from the other direction.

Suddenly, Woof looked up in surprise! A beautiful German shepherd was walking toward him, leading Miss Richards down the street. She was blind and depended totally on her dog Major to help her get around.

Woof had never seen such a wonderful dog in his life! The shepherd was big and powerful. And he was so confident and well-trained. Why, he could have bitten Woof in half if he had wanted.

    Not only was the shepherd beautiful, but he was also a purebred. Woof was only a mutt, and no one even knew who his mother and father were. He stood silently as the big dog walked by with his chest out and his head held high.

    Just then, a car rounded the corner and ran through a big puddle in the road. Before Woof could jump out of the way, the car splashed mud all over him.

Suddenly, Woof felt ugly and foolish. He looked at his own crooked leg and tail. He thought about his bent ear and his rough, shaggy fur covered with mud.

"I sure wish I looked like him," Woof thought to himself looking at the shepherd. "And I wish I had a job like that, leading a blind lady around. That's important work!"

Woof felt terrible as he walked home with his tail between his legs and mud all over his fur.

When Mark and Krissy saw him slinking back into the yard, they laughed out loud.

"You look *so* funny, Woof!" said Krissy.

"Yeah! You don't look so proud now," added Mark.

That night Woof lay on his blanket at the foot of Mark's bed. He couldn't stop thinking about the German shepherd. He still felt ugly and worthless by comparison. He finally went to sleep feeling depressed.

The next morning when Mr. Peterson was leaving for work, he saw Miss Richards coming down the street. This time her dog was not with her and she was using a long white cane to help her walk.

"Hello, Katherine," said Mr. Peterson pleasantly. "How are you this morning?"

The blind woman recognized his voice immediately.

"Hello John," she answered. "I'm afraid I'm not doing very well today. My dog, Major, got sick this morning and had to be taken to the vet. Now he's in the animal hospital, and I'm worried about him. I depend on Major so much to help me. It's really difficult to do errands without him."

"I'm so sorry," said Mr. Peterson. "I wish there was a way I could help." Then he had a great idea!

"Katherine, maybe I *can* help you," he said. "Our dog, Woof, is very smart and dependable. Maybe we could train him to take Major's place for a while."

Miss Richards smiled and clasped her hands together.

"That would be wonderful!" she said. "Is Woof a German shepherd?"

"No," said Mr. Peterson. "We don't know what he is, but the kids sure love him."

"Well, I'm willing to try anything," Miss Richards sighed.

"The children and I will bring Woof over to your house tonight," Mr. Peterson said.

"How kind of you to help me," she replied.

When Mr. Peterson came back inside, he told Mother and the children about his talk with Miss Richards.

"Wow!" shouted Mark. "Woof, the Seeing Eye dog!"

"That's right," said Father. "I think Woof can handle the job just fine. And it would only be until Major gets well."

Mark patted his dog on the head. "You're going to have to work hard to learn this important job," he said. "But I believe you can do it."

Woof didn't understand all their words, but he knew the family was saying something important about him.

That night the Petersons and their dog arrived at Miss Richards' house. Woof knew she was the lady walking with the German shepherd. He also noticed the beautiful dog was not there.

Mr. Peterson hooked a harness around Woof's back, and Woof quickly understood what he was being asked to do. He was supposed to fill in for Major, the Seeing Eye dog!

Within a few days, Woof became comfortable at his new job. He practiced walking up and down the sidewalk with the trainer while the Peterson family watched from their living room. Finally Miss Richards knocked on their front door.

"You have a fine dog," she said, reaching down to stroke his rough fur. "The trainer thinks he's ready to take me to the market."

The Petersons waved good-bye as Woof and Miss Richards headed down the street. Woof was feeling nervous as he led the way, because he knew he was still not as well-trained as Major.

Once he accidently stepped off a curb too soon, and the driver of an on-coming car had to slam on the brakes. Luckily, neither Woof nor Miss Richards was hurt.

Another time he stopped to sniff at a trash can and almost made Miss Richards trip and fall. But she didn't seem to mind. She continued to praise him and tell him what a good job he was doing. By the time they got to the market, Woof was performing almost as well as Major.

When Woof and Miss Richards entered the grocery store, he couldn't believe no one scolded him or asked him to leave. He had never been in a market before. Whenever he went to town with Mark and Krissy, he always had to wait outside buildings for them to come out. This was the first time he had ever been in a public place, and he was excited. After all, only Seeing Eye dogs are allowed in a grocery store.

Woof enjoyed all the wonderful smells around him. He was also amazed at the many rows of food. The smell in the meat section nearly drove him crazy!

Slowly, Woof led Miss Richards up and down the aisles. Even though she was blind, she could recognize foods by the way the packages felt or smelled. She loaded the shopping cart with eggs, milk and butter among other things.

Finally, they came to the produce section. Miss Richards set her purse down on the fruit stand and let go of Woof's harness while she chose ripe oranges and apples.

Suddenly, out of the corner of his eye, Woof saw someone move! Coming toward them were the Harper twins — those mean, trouble-making brothers, Billy and Bobby, who lived next door to the Petersons. The boys had seen Miss Richards' purse sitting on the fruit stand and were waiting to grab it and run. Miss Richards couldn't see the boys sneaking around the tomato bin, but Woof knew exactly what they were up to!

He stiffened his legs, and the hair stood up on the back of his neck.

"What's the matter, Woof?" asked Miss Richards, sensing something was wrong.

Just then Bobby grabbed Miss Richards' purse. Woof lowered his head and growled angrily. A dog's growl does not have human words, but the boys understood what it meant. It said, "Don't you dare take that purse!"

Nervously, the Harper twins looked at each other and began backing away from the dog. They knew Woof could be tough when he wanted. But before they could get away, Woof lunged toward the boys. He scared them so badly that Bobby dropped the purse and the boys ran right into a big bin of tomatoes. What a mess! Tomatoes flew in all directions, splattering on the floor and rolling down the aisle.

In their hurry to escape from Woof, Billy and Bobby Harper slipped on the tomatoes and slid across the floor! By the time they got to the exit their shoes, pants and even their faces were covered in smashed tomatoes. Woof could hardly keep from smiling as he watched the Harper twins run from the store.

After the store manager told Miss Richards what had happened, she patted Woof on the head.

"Thanks for taking care of my purse, Woof" she said. "You're a wonderful friend!"

When they got home from the market, Miss Richards telephoned the Petersons to tell them the story.

"Woof is a very special dog," she said. "I can see why you love him so much."

For the rest of the week, Woof took good care of Miss
Richards. She fed him ground hamburger as a special treat
and brushed his rough fur every day. He was given a warm
bed to sleep in each night. He missed Mark and Krissy, but
he knew how important his job was to Miss Richards. It also
made him feel good to hold a position like Major, the German
shepherd. However, this time Woof didn't feel better than
everyone else, as he did before. He just felt good about being
able to help someone.

Finally, Major returned from the animal hospital, and Woof went home to the Petersons. Mark and Krissy saw a big difference in the way he acted as soon as he arrived. He came to them when he was called and ate all his doggie crunchies. He even brought Mr. Peterson his slippers from the bedroom closet. He became a good ol' dog again, and the family was happy to see the change.

"Woof doesn't seem too proud anymore," said Krissy.

"I think he's happy because he helped someone in need," Mark commented.

"That always makes us feel good about ourselves," said Father. It doesn't really matter how we look or whether or not we are 'purebreds.' What's important is how we treat others!"

The next day Woof invited little Scruffy over to play chase. The two of them rolled in the grass, napped in the shade and ate crunchies from the same dish. Oh, Woof was still a proud dog. He was proud to have a friend like Scruffy. And he was proud to be a member of the Peterson family where everybody felt loved.